A Very Important Day

A Very Important Day

Maggie Rugg Herold

ILLUSTRATED BY
Catherine Stock

MORROW JUNIOR BOOKS   NEW YORK

FOR NORBERT
AND HIS VERY
IMPORTANT DAY
—M.R.H.

THANK YOU MEREDITH FOR
SUGGESTING THIS PROJECT;
THANK YOU MAGGIE FOR
SO ABLY CAPTURING IN WORDS
THE SPIRIT OF THE DAY;
AND THANK YOU JUDGE SWEET
FOR MAKING AN IMPORTANT
DAY TRULY SPECIAL.—C.S.

*N*elia Batungbakal was too excited to sleep. She was looking out her window, listening to music on her Walkman, when she thought she saw snow!

Sure enough, before long the station DJ came on. "It's three A.M. here in New York City, and it's snowing. Four to six inches are expected by noon."

Nelia's mind raced. Imagine, snow on such a very important day. This would never happen in the Philippines. Her son and daughter-in-law and the grandchildren were fast asleep. She would need to awaken them early, to allow extra time for the trip downtown.

"Wake up, Miguel. It's snowing," Rosa Huerta called to her brother. "There are at least two inches on the fire escape."

"All *right*!" said Miguel, bounding from his room. He opened the window and scooped up some snow.

"Close that window," their father ordered. "It's cold in here, and— Miguel, is that snow in your hand?"

"Yes, Papa, the first this year."

"Back outside with it before it melts. And on such a very important day. This would not happen in Mexico, at least not in the south."

"Let's move quickly," urged their mother. "It's six-thirty. We can get an early start downtown."

Veena Patel had just set the table when the doorbell rang. "That will be the children," her husband, Mohandas, said.

But it was their neighbors, the Pitambers. They apologized for stopping by so early. "We were afraid of missing you, and we wanted to wish you well on this very important day."

"Join us for breakfast," said Veena. "Our daughter and her

family will be here any minute. They think we must allow extra time, that the snow will slow us down. That's one worry we never had in India."

The doorbell rang again, and this time it was the children. Everyone gathered quickly at the table, talking eagerly about the special morning ahead.

Out the door and down the steps came the Leonovs—first
Eugenia, then her brother, Lev, followed by their grandfather,
grandmother, mother, and father.

"Snow reminds me of Russia," said their mother.

"I love snow!" exclaimed Eugenia.

Her grandfather stooped, grabbed two handfuls, and threw
them at his grandchildren.

The fight was on.

Just then Mr. Dionetti lobbed a snowball from the door of his corner grocery. "Is this the big day?" he called out. "Are you headed downtown?"

"Yes," answered their father. "This snowball fight is headed for the subway."

"Congratulations!" cried Mr. Dionetti. And tossing a big handful of snow straight up in the air, he crossed the street to shake their hands.

Kostas and Nikos Soutsos were clearing the sidewalk in front of the family restaurant when their mother came out the side door from their apartment above. She was carrying their baby sister, Kiki.

"Kiki, this is snow," said Kostas.

"How do you like it?" Nikos asked.

Kiki seemed puzzled by the flakes that hit her nose.

Their mother laughed. "She'll get used to it, living here. Not like Greece, where it snows maybe once in ten years. But where's your father? We should be on our way."

"He went to make a sign for the door. See, there he is."

"Set those shovels inside, and let's be off," their father called. "And read this sign, everyone. What does it say?"

They chorused together, "Closed for a very important day."

"Finally! There's the bus," said Duong Hao.

He and his older sister, Trinh, brushed snow off each other
and followed their mother on board. It was crowded at first, but
a few stops later they all got seats.

"Here we are," said their mother, "in the middle of a
snowstorm on the most important day since we arrived from
Vietnam—"

Suddenly the driver braked hard.

They were all thrown forward.

"Car skidded at the light and couldn't stop," the driver yelled.
"Everybody okay?"

Fortunately only bundles had landed on the floor.

"That was close," said their mother.

"Yes," said Trinh, "but our driver's good."

Duong nodded. "Maybe he knows that today of all days we just
have to get downtown."

"I love the ferry," said Jorge Báez.

"So do I," agreed his cousin Pedro Jiménez, "especially in snow. Let's go up on deck."

"Not by yourselves, but I'll go with you," said Pedro's father.

"And I'll keep you company," Jorge's father added.

"Me too," begged Jorge's sister. "I want to go outside."

"All right," said her father. "You are old enough."

They went up on deck, leaving the little ones inside with Jorge's mother and aunt.

"I'm so glad this day takes us across the harbor," said Pedro's father. "I never tire of the ride."

"Neither do I," said Jorge's father. "Even in snow, this view is the best in the city. And now we will all remember it as part of the most important day since we came from the Dominican Republic."

Through the narrow streets on the unshoveled sidewalks the Zeng family made their way on foot. Suddenly, from above them, a voice called out.

Yujin's friend Bailong was leaning out the window. "I've been watching for you," he said. "Don't open this until later. Catch!"

Down through the snowflakes came a small brightly wrapped package, straight into Yujin's outstretched hands.

"Thanks, Bailong."

"Thanks for remembering."

"This is such an important day."

"The most important since we arrived from China."

Yujin tucked the package safely inside his coat, and with waves and good-byes the Zengs set off again, heading south.

Jihan Idris and her parents had also left home early to make the trip downtown. Now their subway ride was over, and there was time for breakfast.

"I see a coffee shop ahead," Jihan's mother called out.

"I want to sit at the counter!" Jihan exclaimed.

They entered and sat on three stools, Jihan in the middle.

"I'd like waffles," Jihan told their waitress.

"And I'll have pancakes," said her father. "With coffee and grapefruit juice."

"Scrambled eggs and a toasted bagel, please," said her mother. "With orange juice and tea."

Quickly the waitress was back with their breakfasts. "What brings you out so early on a snowy day like today?" she asked.

"Can you guess?" said Jihan's mother.

"It's the most important day for us since we came from Egypt," said Jihan's father.

"And I'm celebrating with waffles," said Jihan. "I never get them at home."

"There's the courthouse," said Kwame Akuffo to his
wife, Efua, as they rounded a corner, walking fast.

She stopped. "Only two blocks to go. I'll race you to
the steps."

He stopped, too. "Are you crazy?"

"It's not slippery."

"You're on! Ready?"

She nodded.

"On your mark, get set, go!"

And off they dashed, down the sidewalk.

"Tic," Efua declared at the bottom of the steps.

"I used to run in Ghana," Kwame said, "but never in snow."

"Wait," said Efua, taking a camera from her purse.

"Before we go in on this very important day, let's get someone to take our picture."

So they asked a stranger, who gladly obliged, and then hand in hand they climbed the courthouse steps.

As Robert MacTaggart came through the courthouse door, he heard familiar voices calling, "Robert. Over here."

Near the entrance stood his friends Elizabeth and Alan. Each of them gave him a big hug.

"You made it," Robert said. "Thank you so much for coming. I was afraid the snow would stop you."

"Oh, no, not on such an important day," said Elizabeth.

"We were getting worried about *you,* though," said Alan.

Robert chuckled. "A few snowflakes defeat a man from the highlands of Scotland? Come on. Let's find the chamber. It's on this floor."

Leaving relatives and friends to wait in the hall outside, Alvaro Castro, his wife, Romelia, and their children entered the crowded chamber. They were among the last to find seats.

Soon the examiner appeared, and the room became quiet. "When I call your name," he said, "please come forward to receive your certificate."

Many names were called; many people went forward. Then, "Alvaro and Romelia Castro and children Marta, José, and Oscar."

The Castros approached the examiner.

"Please sign here," he said to Alvaro. "And here," he said to Romelia. "These are your papers."

"Thank you," said Alvaro. "This is a proud moment."

The Castros returned to their seats. "The long journey from El Salvador has ended," Romelia whispered to her husband, and he squeezed her hand.

When the examiner had finished, he said, "Please open the door to relatives and friends."

People poured in. There were so many they filled the aisles and lined the walls at the back and sides of the chamber.

"Everyone please rise," said the examiner, and as everyone did, a judge entered the chamber.

"Your Honor," said the examiner, "these petitioners have qualified for citizenship in the United States of America."

"Then," said the judge, "will you repeat after me the oath of citizenship. Let us begin. 'I hereby declare, on oath…'"

"I hereby declare, on oath…"

Echoing the judge phrase by phrase, sentence by sentence, the many voices resounded as one, swearing loyalty to the United States of America.

"Congratulations," said the judge. "Those of you who can be, please be seated."

As the room became quiet again, the judge cleared his throat. "Two hundred nineteen of you from thirty-two countries have become United States citizens here today. You are carrying on a tradition that dates back to the earliest days of our country, for almost all Americans have come here from somewhere else. May citizenship enrich your lives as your lives enrich this country. Welcome. We are glad to have you. This is a very important day."

Everyone then rose and joined the judge in the Pledge of Allegiance.

Family and friends and strangers turned to one another. "Best wishes!" "I'm so happy for you." "You must be so proud." "Isn't it wonderful?" "What a day!" "Let me shake your hand." "Let me give you a kiss." "Let me give you a hug."

Zeng Yujin tore open the package from his friend Bailong. Inside he found small American flags, a dozen or so, enough to share with everyone in his family and with other new citizens surrounding him.

In a wave of excitement, they all made their way out of the chamber, through the hallway, and back to the courthouse door.

"Look!" they exclaimed, everybody talking at once. "The snow has stopped." "The sun is shining." "It will be easy to get home and go on celebrating." "This has become our country on this very important day!"

Glossary of Names

The Philippines
Nelia Batungbakal
    NEL-i-ah bah-TUHNG-bah-KAHL

Mexico
Miguel   mi-GEL
Rosa Huerta   ROE-sah WHERE-tah

India
Veena Patel   VEE-nah PAH-tel
Mohandas   moe-HAHN-dahs
Pitambers   pi-TAHM-buhrs

Russia
Leonovs   lay-OH-nufs
Eugenia   yev-GAY-nee-ah
Lev   LEF

Dionetti   dee-on-ET-ee

Greece
Kostas Soutsos   KOS-tahs SOO-tsose
Nikos   NEE-kose
Kiki   ki-KEE

Vietnam
Duong Hao   ZUNG HAH-oh
Trinh   CHING

Dominican Republic
Jorge Báez   HOR-hay BYE-es
Pedro Jiménez   PAY-droe hee-MEN-es

China
Zeng   DZENG
Yujin   EEOO-JING
Bailong   BYE-LONG

Egypt
Jihan Idris   ji-HAN i-DREES

Ghana
Kwame Akuffo
    KWA-mee ah-KOO-foo
Efua   eh-foo-WAH

Scotland
Robert MacTaggart
    RAH-buhrt mc-TA-guhrt
Elizabeth   e-LIZ-ah-beth
Alan   AL-en

El Salvador
Alvaro Castro   AL-vah-roe CA-stroe
Romelia   roe-MAY-lee-ah
Marta   MAHR-tah
José   hoe-SAY
Oscar   OHS-cahr

The characters in this book are fictional.

Becoming a Citizen

Citizenship is membership in a country. Most people in the United States are citizens because they were born here or because they were born to United States citizens who were living somewhere else. Others become citizens by order of the U.S. court. This is called naturalization.

When U.S. citizens adopt children from other countries, they can apply right away to have their adopted children naturalized. But for others it is a lengthy process.

Before becoming citizens, newcomers to this country must qualify to live here as permanent residents. They can qualify under one of three categories:

- *as relatives of U.S. citizens*
- *as workers who are needed in the U.S. economy*
- *as political refugees*

After five years, or three if married to a U.S. citizen, law-abiding permanent residents over eighteen can apply for citizenship for themselves and their children under eighteen.

There are three steps to applying for citizenship:

- *fill out and submit an application that asks personal questions and requires documents such as a fingerprint chart*
- *take a test called a naturalization examination and appear for an interview*
- *appear for a final court hearing*

The examination tests the applicants' working knowledge of English and knowledge of the history and government of the United States. It includes such questions as "What kind of government does the United States have?" and "What do the stars and stripes on the flag represent?" In the interview, an examiner will ask questions about the application. The examiner will also help the applicant fill out the petition for naturalization, the paper that is actually filed in court.

Once the applicants have passed both the written examination and the interview, they are summoned to a second hearing. There, in a formal ceremony presided over by a judge, they are presented with certificates of naturalization. Then, with right hands raised, the new citizens take the oath of allegiance:

I hereby declare, on oath, that I absolutely and entirely renounce and abjure all allegiance and fidelity to any foreign prince, potentate, state, or sovereignty of whom or which I have heretofore been a subject or citizen; that I will support and defend the Constitution and laws of the United States of America against all enemies, foreign and domestic; that I will bear true faith and allegiance to the same; that I will bear arms on behalf of the United States when required by the law, that I will perform noncombatant service in the Armed Forces of the United States when required by law; that I will perform work of national importance under civilian direction when required by the law; and that I take this obligation freely without any mental reservation or purpose of evasion, so help me God.

The new citizens can vote, serve on juries, compete for all government jobs, travel freely outside the United States, and sponsor parents and brothers and sisters who wish to come live in the United States!

Watercolors were used for the full-color illustrations.   The text type is 17-point Bembo.
Text copyright © 1995 by Maggie Rugg Herold   Illustrations copyright © 1995 by Catherine Stock

Library of Congress Cataloging-in-Publication Data   Herold, Maggie Rugg.   A very important day/by Maggie Rugg Herold; illustrated by Catherine Stock.   p.   cm.   Summary: Two hundred nineteen people from thirty-two different countries make their way to downtown New York in a snowstorm to be sworn in as citizens of the United States.   ISBN 0-688-13065-8 (trade)—ISBN 0-688-13066-6 (library)   [1. Naturalization—Fiction.   2. Emigration and immigration—Fiction.   3. New York (N.Y.)—Fiction.]   I. Stock, Catherine, ill.   II. Title.
PZ7.H43195Ve   1995   [E]—dc20   94-16647   CIP   AC